W9-BHS-472

Flip Flop!

A STICKER BOOK

by Dana Meachen Rau

illustrated by Jana Christy

Random House 🏠 New York

Flip! Flop!

We can't decide.

Swim in the pool?

Or chase the tide?

Do cannonballs?

Or ride the float?

7

Fish from the dock?

Or sail the boat?

Flip! Flop!
What should we do?
Check out the fair?

10

Or try the zoo?

Ride the coaster?

Or win a prize?

CATCH·A·DUCK

Watch fireworks?

14

Or fireflies?

We don't know.

We flip, we flop.

Lick ice cream cone?

Or frozen pop?

Help wash the car?

Or swing and doze?

Sip from a straw?

Or garden hose?

Wear flip-flops?

Or toss the shoes?

Two bare feet are
what we choose.

Dear Parent:

Congratulations! Your child is taking the first steps on an exciting journey. The destination? Independent reading!

STEP INTO READING® will help your child get there. The program offers five steps to reading success. Each step includes fun stories and colorful art. There are also Step into Reading Sticker Books, Step into Reading Math Readers, Step into Reading Phonics Readers, Step into Reading Write-In Readers, and Step into Reading Phonics Boxed Sets—a complete literacy program with something for every child.

Learning to Read, Step by Step!

Ready to Read   Preschool–Kindergarten
• big type and easy words • rhyme and rhythm • picture clues
For children who know the alphabet and are eager to begin reading.

Reading with Help   Preschool–Grade 1
• basic vocabulary • short sentences • simple stories
For children who recognize familiar words and sound out new words with help.

Reading on Your Own   Grades 1–3
• engaging characters • easy-to-follow plots • popular topics
For children who are ready to read on their own.

Reading Paragraphs   Grades 2–3
• challenging vocabulary • short paragraphs • exciting stories
For newly independent readers who read simple sentences with confidence.

Ready for Chapters   Grades 2–4
• chapters • longer paragraphs • full-color art
For children who want to take the plunge into chapter books but still like colorful pictures.

STEP INTO READING® is designed to give every child a successful reading experience. The grade levels are only guides. Children can progress through the steps at their own speed, developing confidence in their reading, no matter what their grade.

Remember, a lifetime love of reading starts with a single step!

To the Fishers
—D.M.R.

For Sophia Elizabeth Jackson
—J.C.

Text copyright © 2011 by Dana Meachen Rau
Illustrations copyright © 2011 by Jana Christy

Published in the United States by Random House Children's Books, a division of Random House, Inc., 1745 Broadway, New York, NY 10019.

Step into Reading, Random House, and the Random House colophon are registered trademarks of Random House, Inc.

Visit us on the Web!
StepIntoReading.com
www.randomhouse.com/kids

Educators and librarians, for a variety of teaching tools, visit us at
www.randomhouse.com/teachers

Library of Congress Cataloging-in-Publication Data
Rau, Dana Meachen.
Flip flop! / by Dana Meachen Rau ; illustrated by Jana Christy.
   p. cm. — (Step into reading. A step 1 book)
Summary: Rhyming text explores the many options that summer presents to two best friends, from swimming in a pool versus swimming in the sea, to wearing flip flops versus going barefoot.
ISBN 978-0-375-86583-1 (trade pbk.) — ISBN 978-0-375-96583-8 (lib. bdg.)
[1. Stories in rhyme. 2. Summer—Fiction. 3. Choice—Fiction.] I. Christy, Jana, ill. II. Title.
PZ8.3.R232Fli 2011
[E]—dc22   2010024998

Printed in the United States of America
10 9 8 7 6 5 4 3